Chicken Little

A Tale about Common Sense

Retold by Sarah Albee
Illustrated by Atelier Philippe Harchy

Reader's Digest Young Families

Once upon a time, Chicken Little was scratching in her yard, searching for tasty seeds to eat. Suddenly an acorn dropped from an oak tree and—plink!—landed on her head.

"Squaaaaawk!" said Chicken Little. "The sky is falling! A bit of it just fell on my head! I must go and warn the king!"

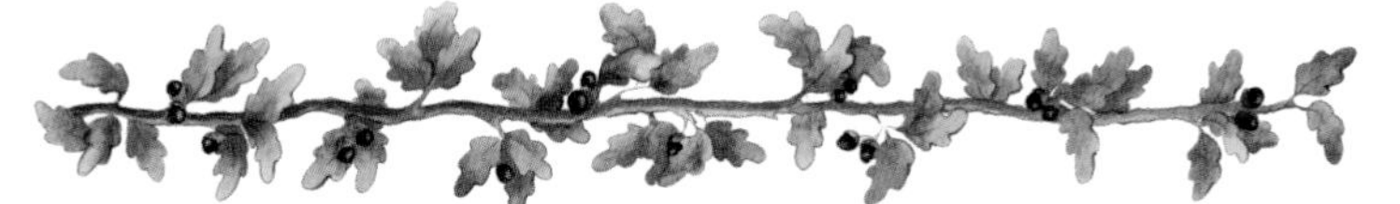

Chicken Little hurried out of the yard and into the lane.

"Where are you going, Chicken Little?" asked Henny Penny.

"The sky is falling!" replied Chicken Little. "I am off to warn the king!"

"May I come too?" asked Henny Penny.

Chicken Little agreed at once, and off they went.

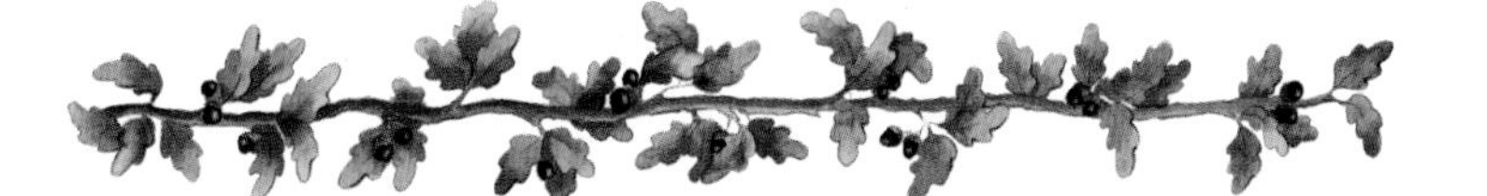

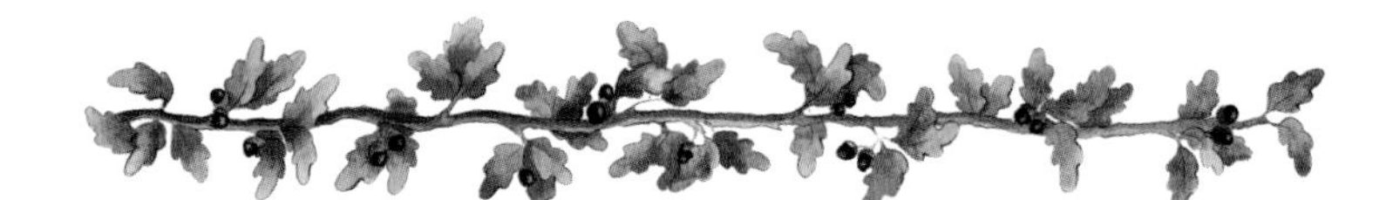

"Where are you two going in such a hurry?" asked Cocky Locky, who was resting atop a fence.

"The sky is falling!" replied Henny Penny. "We are off to warn the king!"

"How do you know?" asked Cocky Locky.

"Chicken Little told me!" replied Henny Penny.

"A piece of the sky fell on me just a few moments ago!" said Chicken Little.

Cocky Locky, who wanted to see the king, decided to join them. Together they continued down the lane.

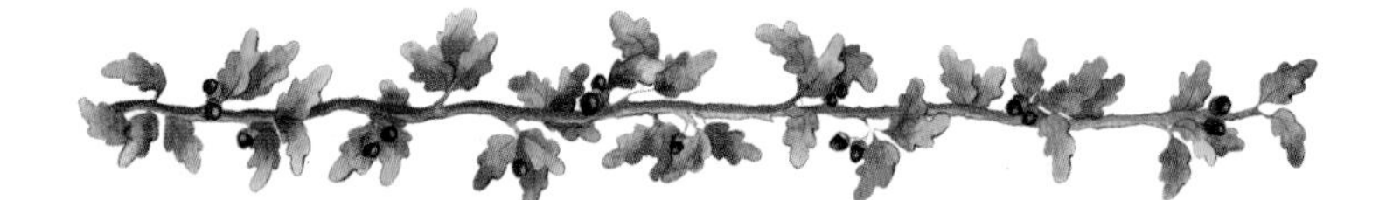

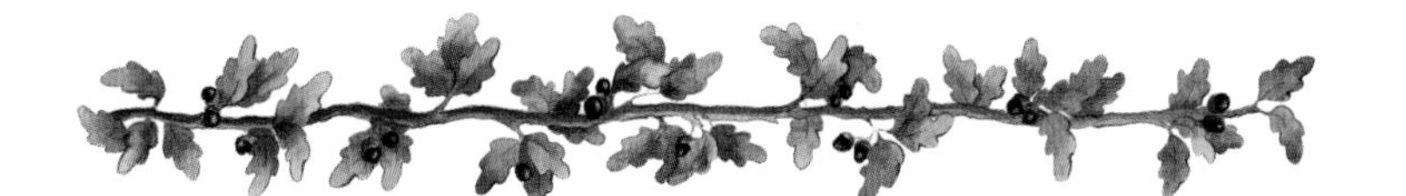

"Where are you three going?" called Ducky Lucky.

"The sky is falling!" said Cocky Locky. "Henny Penny told me so!"

"Chicken Little told me so!" said Henny Penny.

"A bit of sky fell on my head!" explained Chicken Little. "Come along with us! We must warn the king!"

So Ducky Lucky joined the group.

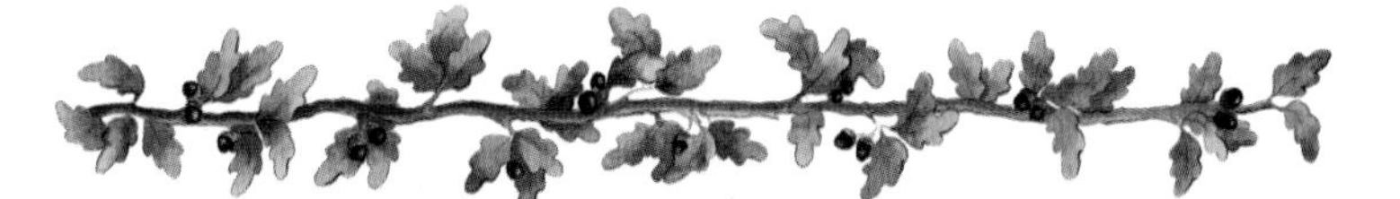

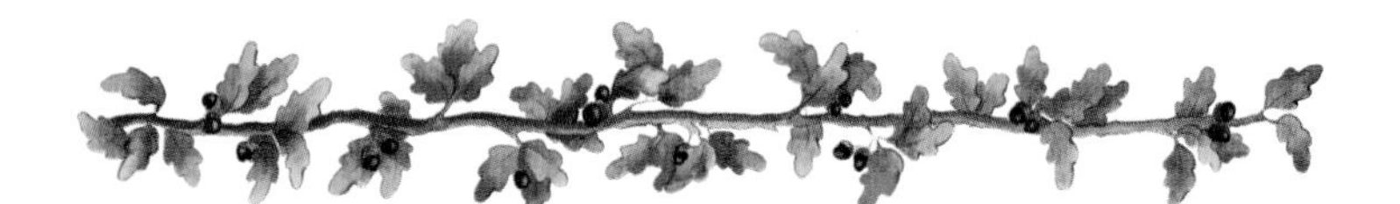

"Where are you four going in such a hurry?" Goosey Loosey wanted to know.

"The sky is falling!" replied Ducky Lucky. "Cocky Locky just told me!"

"Well, Henny Penny told me so!" said Cocky Locky.

"And Chicken Little told me so!" said Henny Penny.

"A bit of the sky fell down on my head!" said Chicken Little. "We are off to warn the king. Would you like to come along?"

Goosey Loosey did want to come along. Off they all dashed down the lane.

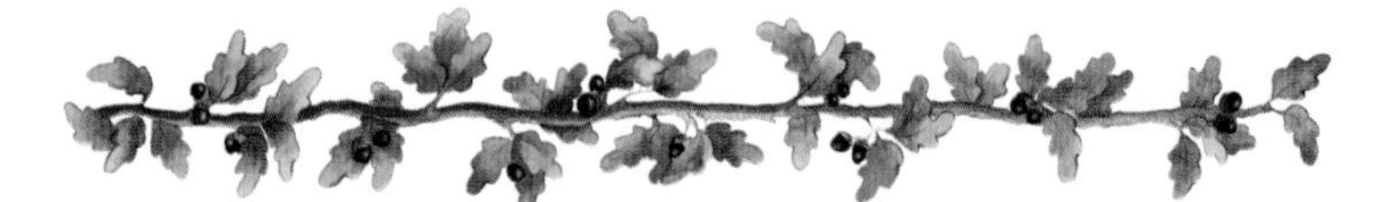

Next they met Turkey Lurkey. "Where are all of you going?" he asked them curiously.

"The sky is falling!" said Goosey Loosey. "We must warn the king!"

Turkey Lurkey looked worriedly up at the sky. "May I come with you?" he asked them.

"Certainly!" they all cried together, and off the group dashed down the lane.

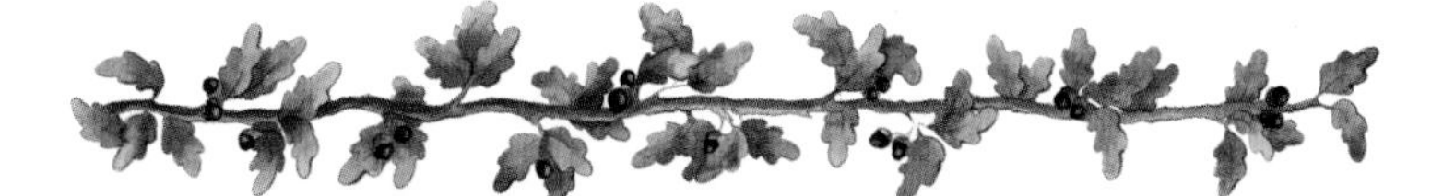

Foxy Loxy leaned against a tree, watching the group run down the lane. "Where are you all going in such a hurry?" he inquired with a sly smile.

"To warn the king!" panted Turkey Lurkey.

"Yes, before it's too late!" added Goosey Loosey.

"Because the sky is falling!" puffed Ducky Lucky.

"Henny Penny told me!" said Cocky Locky.

"Chicken Little felt it fall!" huffed Henny Penny.

"Yes! Some sky fell on my head!" Chicken Little told the fox.

"Is that so?" said Foxy Loxy. "Well, I know a shortcut. Why don't you follow me?" he suggested.

The tired travelers gratefully followed Foxy Loxy.

The animals didn't realize it, but Foxy Loxy led them to his den. Quick as a flash, he leaped at the group. They scattered in fright, but not before Foxy Loxy caught Goosey Loosey in his paws. Just as he was about to gobble her up, a tree branch broke and fell on his head with a crash.

"It appears the sky really is falling!" mumbled the dazed fox, releasing Goosey Loosey.

The others grabbed Goosey Loosey and ran away as fast as they could. They hid behind a stone wall and breathed a giant sigh of relief.

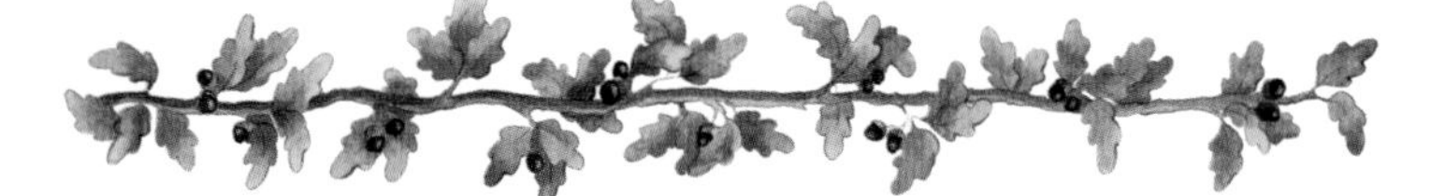

At that moment, the king and his two attendants galloped into view. They stopped when they saw the group of animals by the wall.

"Your Majesty! Your Majesty! We were just on our way to warn you at great peril to ourselves that the sky is falling!" cried Chicken Little. "A bit of it fell on my head this very day!"

The king leaned down and plucked a tiny acorn from the feathers of the little chicken's head. "It was only an acorn," he said to her gently. "Next time, think about the situation before running off and alarming everyone!"

And so the group returned home, a bit wiser than before.

Famous Fables, Lasting Virtues
Tips for Parents

Now that you've read Chicken Little, *use these pages as a guide to teach your child the virtues in the story. By talking about the story and its message and engaging in the suggested activities, you can help your child develop good judgment and a strong moral character.*

About Common Sense

Why is the story of Chicken Little so appealing to children? One reason is that her literal interpretation of events is very childlike. As any parent knows, young children are very literal. They might genuinely believe that there is a tiny person speaking to us from inside the radio or that a feathery snowfall is the result of angels having a pillow fight.Teaching children about cause and effect and helping them to develop thinking skills are essential goals for parents. Here are a few ways to nurture the virtue of common sense in your child while preserving her sense of wonder and imagination.

1. *Cause and effect.* Raise the topic of cause and effect whenever you can. "If I bang this egg against the bowl, what will happen? What will happen if I leave the ice cube on the counter?" When possible, demonstrate the outcome. The more knowledge your child can acquire through daily living, the more he will understand the world around him, thus developing his common sense.

2. *Encourage questions.* Praise your child for asking questions. Help your child use logic and common sense to figure out the answers before immediately providing the answers. If your child asks why the dog wags its tail, for example, ask her how she thinks the dog is feeling. "Does he look happy or sad? What are some ways *you* show how you feel with your body?"

3. *Story time, teaching time.* Use some of story time to help your child develop critical thinking skills. As you read a book to your child, think out loud about the events in the story. For example, you might predict an outcome ("I bet he's going to get into trouble if he does..."). Or draw a conclusion ("His mother's face looks..."). Or ask a question ("Why did he want to...").